THE EARTH BOOK

TODD PARR

Megan Tingley Books
LITTLE, BROWN AND COMPANY
NEW YORK BOSTON

To my mom and dad, for putting me on Earth.
To Liz and Gerry for going to Las Vegas and to
Megan for asking me if I had ever thought about
writing children's books.

Special thanks to Liza and Fatimah.

Love, Todd

I take care of the earth because I know I can do little things every day to make a BIG difference.

I use both sides of the paper

and bring my own bags
to the market because...
LOCAL
MARKET

I love the trees

and I want the owls to have a place to live.

I turn off the faucet
while I brush my teeth

and use less water
for my baths because...

I love the fish

and I wan[illegible] the oceans [illegible]o stay blue.

I take the school bus

and ride my bike because...

I love the stars and I want the air

to be clear so I can see them sparkle.

I try to eat every bite on my plate

and save my leftovers because...

I love watching things grow

and I want there to be
enough food for everyone.

I remember to turn off the lights

and shu the refrigera or
to save energy because...

I love the polar bears

and I want the snowmen to stay cool.

I throw garbage in the trash can

and recycle glass, aluminum, paper, and plastic because...

I love to walk barefoot in the grass

and I don't want to move to Mars!

Most of all, I help take care

of the earth because . . .

I want us ALL to be happy and healthy!

10 Ways I Can

1. 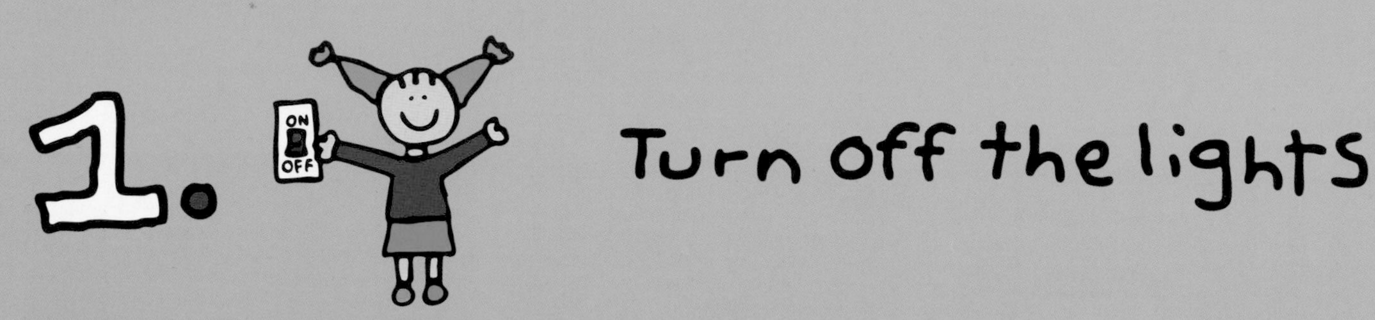

Turn off the lights

2. 

RECYCLE!

3.  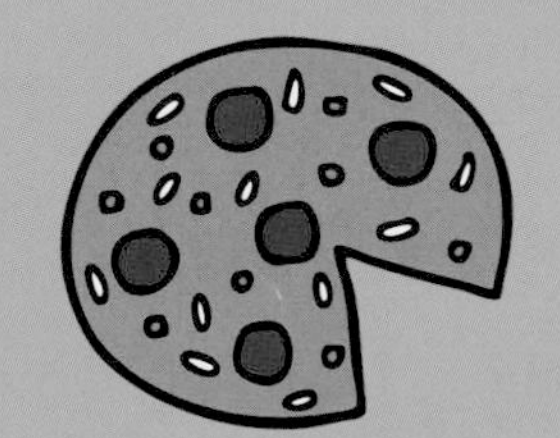
Save my leftovers

4.  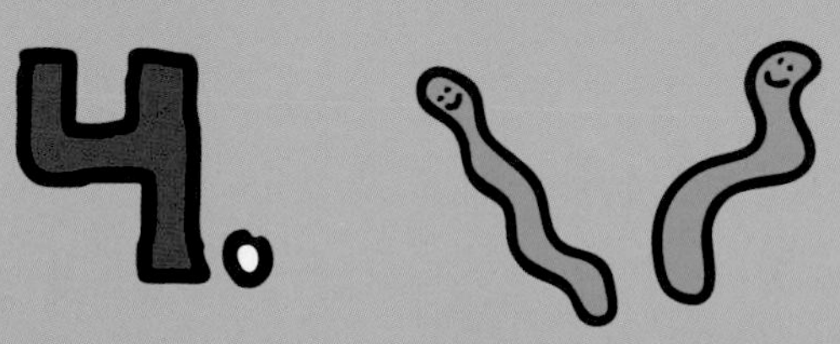
Be nice to the worms

5. 

Share a book

Help the EARTH

6. Plant a tree

7. Use both sides of the paper

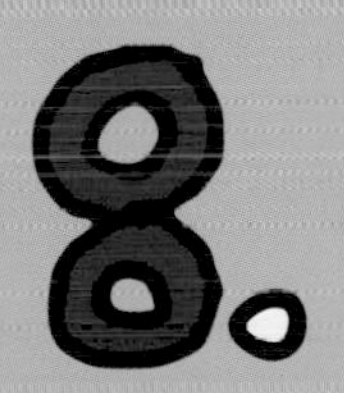

8. Save water

9. Clean up trash

10. Put my underwear in the freezer when it's hot

Every one of us can help protect the earth and make it feel good.

Remember: if we take care of it, it will take care of us.

Love, Todd

Todd Parr has inspired and empowered children around the world with his bold images and positive messages. He is the bestselling author of more than forty books. He lives in Berkeley, California. You can find him online at toddparr.com, on Facebook, or on Twitter.

Also by Todd Parr:

For a complete list of all
Todd's books and more information, please visit
toddparr.com

Little, Brown and Company
Hachette Book Group
1290 Avenue of the Americas, New York, NY 10104
Visit us at LBYR.com

Little, Brown and Company is a division of Hachette Book Group, Inc.
The Little, Brown name and logo are trademarks of Hachette Book Group, Inc.

The publisher is not responsible for websites (or their content) that are not owned by the publisher.

This book is printed with nontoxic soy inks.

First Edition: March 2010

Library of Congress Cataloging-in-Publication Data

Parr, Todd. The EARTH book / Todd Parr. p. cm.
ISBN 978-0-316-04265-9
1. Earth—Juvenile literature. I. Title.
QB631.4.P387 2009
333.72—dc22 2008047562

ISBN: 978-0-316-04265-9

PRINTED IN CHINA

20 19 18 17 16 15 14 13 12 11

APS